FUTUREWORD PUBLISHING

Copyright ©2012 by Yvonne E. Lovell   All Rights Reserved

ISBN 9780615726304 *A Gift For Mrs. Peaches*

Illustrated by Tata Jariashvili

First Print Edition 11.17.12

Printed in the USA

11.17.12

I dedicate this book to my Mom, Blanche Lenoue who struggled in her teen years to take care of all my needs. I never doubted her love. We would sit at my play table and chair set to eat our dinner after she came home tired from working at the nursing home. Thank you, Mom, for teaching me to love others and to care for their needs.

Luke 10:27 He answered: "'Love the Lord your God with all your heart and with all your soul and with all your strength and with all your mind'; and, 'Love your neighbor as yourself.'" NASB

To

Love is a word we say, but real love is what we do for other people. May God bless your life with love over flowing.

Yvonne E. Lovell

A Gift For Mrs. Peaches

written by

Yvonne E. Lovell

pictures by Jariashvili

Mrs. Scamper the squirrel was worried about Mrs. Peaches. She jumped from tree to tree, scrambled across rocks, and dashed across meadows on her way to Theodore's house.

By the time she reached Theodore's house she was frazzled and out of breath. She pounded on his front door and prayed that Theodore was at home.

Theodore greeted her at the door with a happy smile. "Hello, Mrs Scamper! You look worn out. Come in and sit for a while."

Theodore led Mrs. Scamper to a kitchen chair. She was chattering so fast that he thought, *Something must be seriously wrong for her to be so upset.* He held up a paw and said, "Please, slow down. I can't understand you when you talk so fast. Is something wrong with your family?"

Mrs. Scamper shook her head 'no' in reply to her family. Then she began to try to explain a little slower.

"Mrs. Peaches is sick. She says she has bad luck and will never get well. She also says her bad luck spreads to everyone she's near. Oh, Theodore, I've got to do something that will help her. What am I to do?"

Taking a deep breath, she continued, "I know your love works magic because you spread it everywhere you go."

"You need to calm down a little," soothed Theodore, "And have a cup of hot apple cider. We need to trust God to help us work this out."

"You're right. We all need to trust God and have faith," Mrs. Scamper sighed. "That's the problem. I don't think Mrs. Peaches knows this."

Theodore put the kettle on the stove. Then he placed a bowl of mixed acorns, sunflower seeds, and peanuts on the table.

"Oh, thank you for remembering my favorite treats," Mrs. Scamper said as she paced back and forth.

By the time the cider was ready Mrs. Scamper and Theodore were seated at the table. Theodore said, "Alright! Now, let's put our heads together and decide what we can do to help your friend."

Mrs. Scamper relaxed in Theodore's bright cozy kitchen. She slowly munched on the delightful nuts. Theodore poured honey over a bun and took a bite. They sat quietly for a few minutes, eating and thinking about what they could do to cheer up Mrs. Peaches.

Finally, Theodore broke the silence. "We need to rid Mrs. Peaches of the belief that she has–and brings–bad luck."

"How can we remove something we can't see, or give someone luck?" Mrs. Scamper replied. "I'm confused."

"Don't worry, we'll help Mrs. Peaches. It's love we need to show her," Theodore replied.

"Of course! You're a loving bear. Your love spreads everywhere! But what can we do for luck, if love's the answer?" she asked. "You can't hand someone luck. It can't be done. I thought about a four-leaf-clover. Some people believe they get lucky when they find one."

"That's a myth," Theodore pointed out. His eyes caught a movement outside the window. It was Mr. Hare hopping past.

Theodore jumped up from his chair, smiling. He led Mrs. Scamper to the front door. "I've got a good idea, but it will take the love of everyone we know. You gave me the idea."

"You're talking in riddles, Theodore. What did I say?"

"What do you think of when it's St. Patrick's Day?" Theodore asked.

Mrs. Scamper was puzzled. "A shamrock . . . a four-leaf-clover, of course. But how will a shamrock help my friend if it's only a myth?"

"You said people *believe* the Shamrock is lucky. Believing is the key,'" said Theodore. "Mrs. Peaches believes it can help her. If Mrs. Peaches discovers she has **_luck_** and **love** too, she will feel better soon."

"That's wonderful, Theodore. But where are we going to find a four-leaf-clover? I wouldn't even know where to look for clover."

"We're going for help. Mr. Hare should be an expert on finding clover." Theodore replied.

Theodore and Mrs. Scamper continued on until they found Mr. Hare nibbling clover out in the center of the field.

"Hello Theodore and Mrs. Scamper," Mr. Hare smiled. "Isn't this a beautiful day? The sun feels good. I might stretch out and enjoy it. What brings you out this way?"

Mrs. Scamper started searching for a four-leaf clover from the clovers in Mr. Hare's arms.

Mrs. Scamper started to chatter nervously. Theodore laughed, and told Mr. Hare, "Mrs. Peaches is ill. She believes she has no luck. We thought you could help us find a four-leaf clover. We think this may cheer her up."

Mr. Hare sat down. He rubbed his chin and lowered both ears in thought. Suddenly, he hopped up, twitched his nose and said, "I remember a long time ago I found one. But they are very rare. We better hurry before it gets dark. Follow me!"

They followed Mr. Hare to a field on Mrs. Peaches's land and began searching for the four-leaf clover. After searching for over an hour, Mr. Hare hopped up, twitched his nose and shouted, "I found it. I found it."

Theodore teased Mr. Hare, "If you don't stop jumping around, you might lose our gift. Although this four-leaf clover won't bring Mrs. Peaches luck, it will show her our love. That's what is important."

"Let's hurry! It's getting late." Mrs. Scamper said. She lead the way to Mrs. Peaches's backyard.

Mr. Peaches was the first one to spot the trio as they reached the back gate. "We have company, my dear," he said.

Mrs. Peaches smiled at Mrs. Scamper as she pulled the shawl tightly around her shoulders.

"Where have you been?" Mrs. Peaches asked. "I missed your morning visit. Who are your friends?"

"They're your friends, too. They helped me find a gift for you," said Mrs. Scamper. "This is Theodore and Mr. Hare."

"Mrs. Scamper told me you were a magic bear, Theodore. What kind of magic or tricks do you do?"

He laughed. "I don't do tricks. My magic is spreading love to everyone I meet."

"That's kind of hard because not everyone is lovable."

"I believe we need to give our love, freely, before we can receive love back. I believe that's what keeps love flowing," said Theodore.

By this time Mrs. Scamper was chattering and bouncing around making everyone laugh. She wanted to give Mrs. Peaches her gift.

Theodore laughed and said, "Mrs. Scamper, you really should give Mrs. Peaches **_your_** gift first."

That stopped Mrs. Scamper in her tracks. She peeked between her paws to make sure the four-leaf clover was still intact.

She hopped up to the swing next to Mrs. Peaches and said, "We want to give you a symbol of luck. We also give you our love, which will never wilt or fade away."

Mr. Hare gave a toothy smile, wiggled his ears, and said, "We came to make you happy. We want to give you a gift that will remind you that you are lucky."

"We help each other. Whenever someone is sick, we do something kind or helpful to cheer them up," Theodore lovingly reassured Mrs. Peaches.

Mrs. Peaches smiled as big tears formed in her eyes.

Tears slowly flowed down Mrs. Peaches's cheeks. She began to smile. "Love, freely given, is a precious gift and one to treasure. I thank God for my new friends," she said in a soft, choked voice.

About The Author

Yvonne E. Lovell was born in Mt. Vernon, Washington on November 28, 1938. She moved to Tacoma, Washington with her mother and grandparents when she was two years old and grew up there.

Yvonne started a business in ceramics with a friend, then ventured out on her own. The day she applied for a business license she found a penny and named her shop **Lucky Penny Ceramics.** After fifteen years of selling and teaching ceramics classes, she took an interest in floral art. That worked out so well that she changed the name to **Lucky Penny Floral** and stayed in the flower business until 1995 when she decided she would close the shop. In 1996 she went to Pierce College to learn how to use a computer. She decided to try for her GED and was awarded that in the same year.

Yvonne enjoyed learning so much that she decided to take reading and writing classes. Her instructors had a big influence on bringing out her writing talent. The next thing she discovered was she liked to journal and write poems to express her inner heart. But most of all she liked to write stories for children because she said, "It makes me feel like a child again and I like to get into each character role."

Yvonne was introduced to Cheryl Haynes, Publisher at FutureWord by copywriter and best selling author, Kristine M. Smith who was contracted to edit the work. *A Gift For Mrs. Peaches* struck home to the publisher and the book was put into production.

Yvonne lives in Tacoma, Washington with her husband, James. They have two children, Debra Diane, and Jeffery Lynn, three grandchildren, and five great-grandchildren. She calls them her treasured gems from God in her golden years.

About The Illustrator

Tata Jariashvili was born on July 26th, 1983, in Tbilisi, Georgia. After graduating from Tbilisi State Art academy in 2006, she began illustrating children's books and puzzles for Georgia's leading houses and acquired several international clients as well.

Yvonne E. Lovell saw her artwork displayed on Elance and sent her an inquiry. The artwork was submitted to FutureWord Publishing along with Yvonne's manuscript which was passed along to Valerie Bouthyette, the head of children's books, for approval.

Tata says, "All my family members are artists so my career choice wasn't a surprise for them. I work in any style illustrations."

Made in the USA
Charleston, SC
30 December 2012